This book belongs to

_____

Published by Advance Publishers
© 1998 Disney Enterprises, Inc.
All rights reserved. Printed in the United States.
No part of this book may be reproduced or copied in any form
without the written permission of the copyright owner.

Written by Lisa Ann Marsoli
Illustrated by Peter Emslie and David Scott Smith
Produced by Bumpy Slide Books

ISBN: 1-57973-002-7

10 9 8 7 6 5 4 3 2 1

Mowgli liked living in the Man-village. It wasn't the carefree life he had known in the jungle with Baloo, but after his chores were done, he had plenty of time to explore and play with his new friends.

Today he had entertained the children with the story of how Baloo dressed up like a monkey and danced with King Louie. How everyone laughed! So did Mowgli.

The more he thought about the buddies he had left behind in the jungle, the more Mowgli missed them. "I don't see any reason why I can't go back for a visit," Mowgli said to himself. "Imagine how surprised Baloo and Bagheera will be to see me."

Next Mowgli asked the chief of the village for permission to make the journey.

The chief agreed, so Mowgli tied some food up in a large palm leaf, took a hollow gourd for a drinking cup, and headed off on his trip.

Mowgli strolled through the jungle he knew so well. He answered the calls of a parrot, climbed a small mountain of boulders, and skipped rocks across a stream. After a while, he stopped to have something to eat. Then he leaned against a tree to have an afternoon snooze.

The Man-cub dreamed that Shere Khan was stalking him through the jungle. In his dream, he never saw the tiger's face. But he could hear the plants rustling behind him, and knew the beast was close by.

Mowgli awoke to the sound of shaking leaves. "Shere Khan!" he thought to himself, feeling just a little scared. When he had lived in the jungle, he had not been afraid of the tiger. But now he knew it was smart to fear certain creatures.

He imagined that he saw a flash of orange and black stripes near the rocks just beyond him.

Mowgli took a deep breath, rubbed his eyes, and looked around him. Everything appeared just as it had before he had fallen asleep. "That's what happens when you have too many bananas before a nap," Mowgli said with a chuckle.

Mowgli picked up his parcel of food and went over to the river to wash. As he splashed the cold water on his face, he heard a low moan behind him. He turned and saw a tigress slouching toward the cover of some bushes.

"So it wasn't a dream, after all," Mowgli thought. He stayed still and quiet, watching the tigress's slow, painful movements. "No tigress I've ever seen walks like that," he decided. "She must be hurt."

Even though Mowgli knew it might be dangerous, he slowly approached the tigress. When he was close enough for her to catch his scent, she raised her head out of the bushes to investigate. She growled, hoping this would be enough to scare the boy away.

Mowgli stopped where he stood. "My name is Mowgli," he said, "and I was just wondering — are you all right?"

"Leave now or I'll have you for my dinner," answered the tigress. She tried to sound fierce, but her voice was tired.

Mowgli crept a little closer to the bush. Now he could see that the tigress had a litter of cubs. Alarmed, the tigress tried to raise herself up. She knew she was too weak to truly frighten the boy. Not knowing what else to do, she said, "Please leave me alone. If you harm me, my cubs will have no one to care for them."

"But I don't want to harm you. I want to help you," replied Mowgli.

"Help me?" answered the tigress. "But men kill tigers with their guns and their fire."

"Don't worry," Mowgli reassured her. "I don't have either one of those."

Just then, one of the cubs became curious and bounded over to Mowgli. Mowgli smiled at his boldness and scratched him behind the ears.

The tigress relaxed just a little. Maybe this boy truly didn't mean them any harm.

"My name is Sheba," she said softly.

Mowgli sat down on the ground opposite Sheba, and within seconds all of the cubs were climbing in his lap. "How did you get hurt?" Mowgli asked their mother.

"A few days ago I was hunting for food," Sheba began. "I slipped and fell down a steep cliff. I was badly injured, and it took me a long time to climb back up the rocks. But I kept going because I knew I had to return to my cubs."

"Then what?" Mowgli wanted to know.

"I've been resting in these bushes ever since, unable to hunt," Sheba replied. "Luckily, my cubs don't eat meat yet. They are still happy to drink their fill of milk."

"Do you feel any better?" Mowgli asked.

"My bruises are healing, but I am very tired," Sheba admitted. "I haven't been able to sleep. Since I can't protect my cubs, I need to make sure they are hidden and safe when danger nears."

Mowgli dared to inch a bit closer to the proud mother tigress. "I still think I can help you if you'll let me," he offered.

Sheba was taken by surprise. "I still don't understand," she told him. "Why are you being so kind?"

Mowgli smiled. "When I was a baby," he began, "a wolf family adopted me and raised me.

Then when I was older, my friends Baloo and Bagheera took care of me and protected me from Shere Khan. Later, when I arrived at the Man-village, the strangers there welcomed me. I have learned that we all need to look after each other in the jungle."

"All right, then," Sheba agreed. "What is your plan?"

"Before we talk anymore, I think you should eat," Mowgli said. He unwrapped his parcel of food and offered her what remained.

Then he took the hollow gourd he carried with him and ran down to the river. As he bent to fill it, the cubs came racing after him and jumped on him with all their might. Mowgli lost his balance and fell straight into the river. The cubs thought this was a wonderful game and joined him in the shallow water.

"Hey!" cried Mowgli, pretending to scold them. "Cut that out!"

As Sheba watched Mowgli playing with her cubs, she began to trust him just a little more. And she was grateful when he brought her the gourd of cool water to drink. Maybe he would be able to help her after all.

"I am going to visit some friends of mine," Mowgli explained. "They don't live far from here. Why don't you and your cubs come with me? You can stay with them for as long as it takes you to get better. And they could watch over your cubs while you rest. They won't mind. After all, they used to take care of me!"

The cubs crowded around their mother. It was clear they liked this strange boy who didn't behave at all like a young Man should. Finally Sheba decided that, like it or not, she had no choice. For the good of her cubs, she had to follow the boy. But she had one last question.

"Why are you so different from other Men?"
she wondered.

"Maybe it's because I'm not a Man, but a Man-
cub," Mowgli answered. And then he laughed and
howled just the way the wolves had taught him.

Meanwhile, in a clearing in the jungle, Baloo and Bagheera were just saying good-bye to Rama, his mate, and their new litter of puppies.

"Those pups remind me of how young and helpless Mowgli was when I first came across him," Baloo remembered. "I sure do miss him."

"I miss him, too," Bagheera agreed. "Although I'll never forget all the trouble he caused when we tried to take him to the Man-village!"

"He's probably so grown up, he could scare off Shere Khan all by himself."

Bagheera shook his head. "Oh, Baloo, don't be ridiculous! He's only been gone a month!"

Later that afternoon, Mowgli appeared out of the bushes.

"Little Buddy!" exclaimed Baloo. "We were just talkin' about ya! I knew one day you'd come back to pay your old Papa Bear a —"

Baloo froze in fear as he caught sight of Sheba and her cubs coming up behind Mowgli. "Look out!" he warned.

"It's all right, Baloo," Mowgli said. "These are my new friends." Then he explained why he had brought Sheba and her offspring for a visit.

"Mowgli, have you taken leave of your senses?" asked Bagheera. "Don't you know that all tigers are like Shere Khan? You can't trust them for a moment. Who knows what they'll do when your back is turned?"

"I think we should go now," Sheba said to Mowgli. "I knew this was a bad idea." She tried to gather up her cubs, but they were all having too much fun learning how to spar from Baloo.

"I think you should rest awhile first," Mowgli suggested.

Exhausted, the tigress agreed. She lay down
under a tree nearby, keeping one eye on her cubs.

Soon Bagheera, Baloo, and Mowgli were sharing stories of recent adventures and remembering their past adventures together. After a while, Mowgli thought it was time to bring his new friend into the group. "Why don't you tell everyone how you —" Mowgli began. But Sheba was fast asleep.

By the time Sheba awoke, Baloo and Bagheera had decided the cubs couldn't possibly return to the jungle with an injured mother. And by the next day, they realized that not all tigers were like Shere Khan. They happily took care of the noble tigress and her family until she was strong again.

As she prepared to leave, Sheba said gratefully, "Thank you for your kindness. If there is anything I can ever do for you, please send word and I promise I will come."

Because lending a hand is what good neighbors — be they tigers, bears, panthers, or Man-cubs — do.

Mowgli met a tigress and
He could have run in fear;
If she had been stronger,
She might not have let him near.
Soon between these strangers
A seed of friendship grew;
Like many so-called enemies,
They shared more than they knew.